SCP
INSPIRED ARTWORK

BY CHRISTOPHER TUPA

Secure. Contain. Protect.

ctupa.com

Copyright 2020 by Christopher Tupa. All rights reserved.

Content relating to the SCP Foundation, including the SCP Foundation logo,
is licensed under Creative Commons Sharealike 3.0 and all concepts
originate from http://www.scp-wiki.net and its authors.
This artwork, being derived from this content, is hereby also released
under Creative Commons Sharealike 3.0.

SCP 3199

SCP 096

SCP 1128

SCP 3008

SCP 1010

SCP 3166

SCP 4666

SCP 1678A

SCP 1471

SCP 2256

SCP 054

SCP 088

SCP 1730

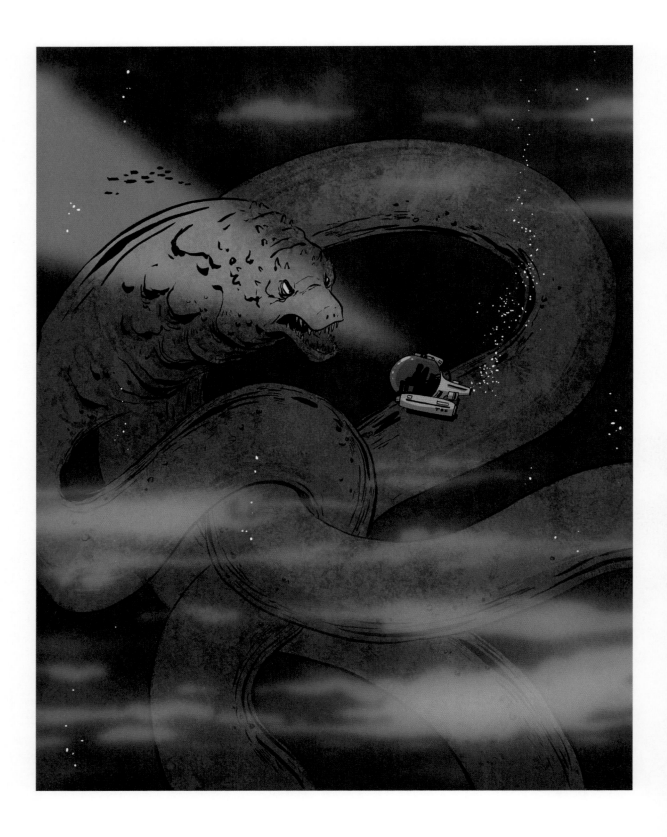

SCP 3000

SCP 040

SCP 682

SCP 002

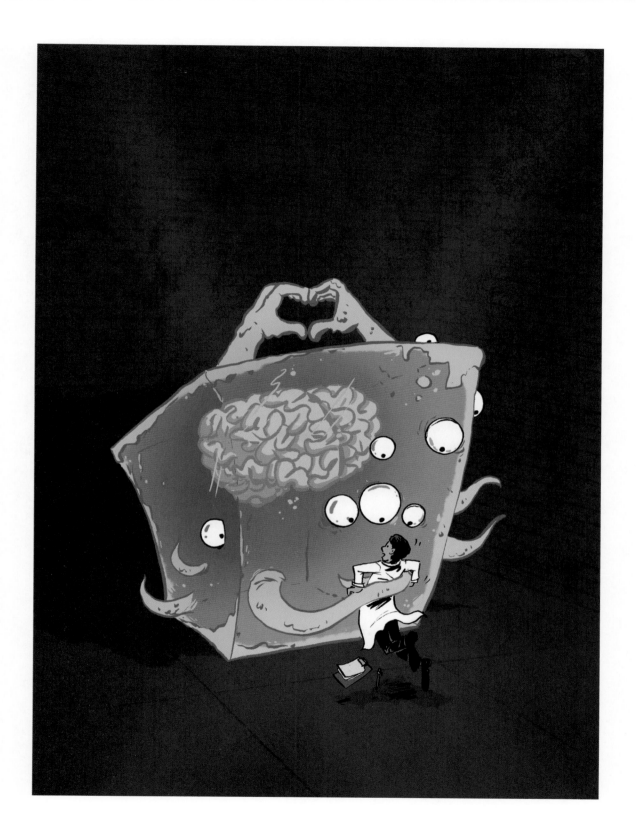

SCP 1983

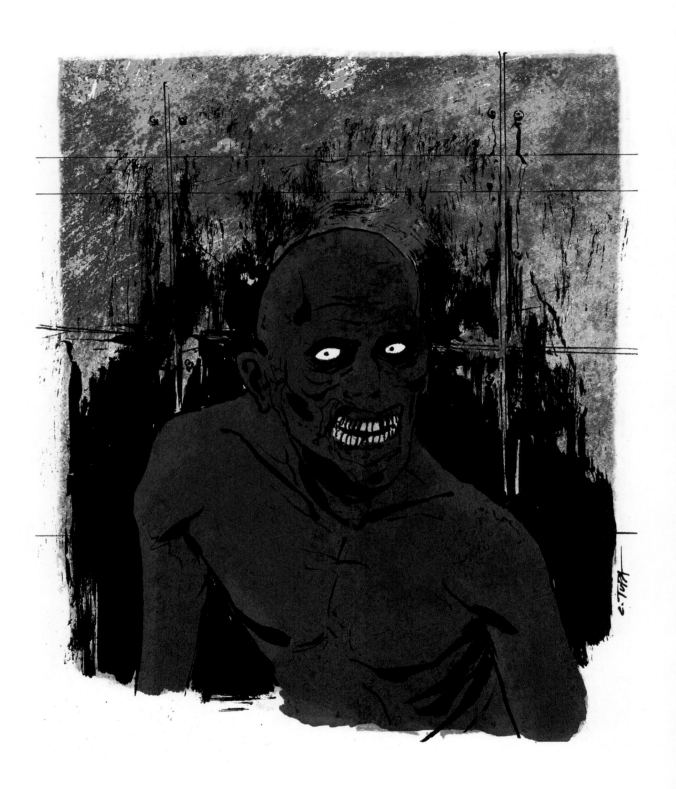

SCP 106

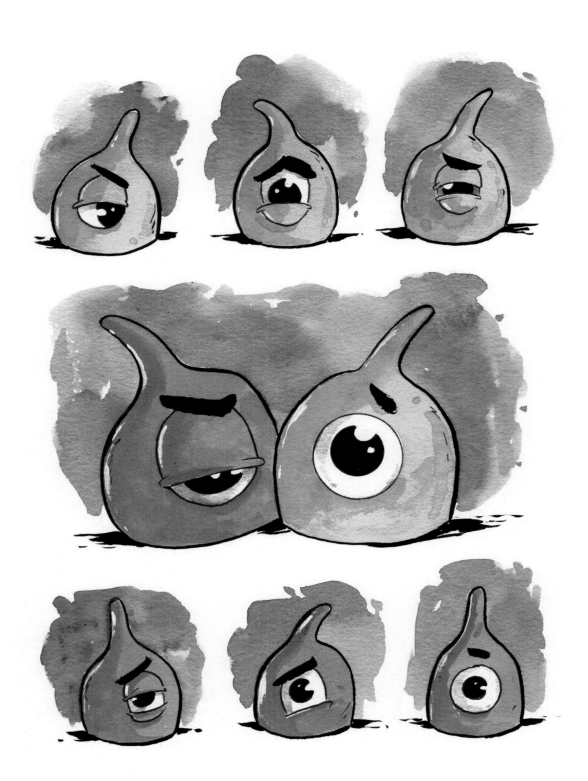

SCP 993

SCP 2521

SCP 939

SCP 610

SCP 527

SCP 650

Secure. Contain. Protect.

CTUPA.COM

Printed in Great Britain
by Amazon

12901856R00025